Puppies on Parade

By Sierra Harimann
Illustrated by The Artifact Group

SCHOLASTIC INC.

ISBN 978-0-545-59211-6

Published by Scholastic Inc. SCHOLASTIC and associated logos are trademarks and/or registered trademarks of Scholastic Inc.
Lexile is a registered trademark of MetaMetrics, Inc.

12 11 10 9 8 7 6 5 4 3 2   14 15 16 17 18/0
Designed by Angela Jun
Printed in the U.S.A.   40
First printing, March 2014

Sammy was headed to dance class one day in early March. She held on to her hat with one paw to keep it from blowing off her head.

"*Whoa!*" she barked. "What a windy day!"

1

First Annual
Puppyville
St. Patrick's Day
Parade

Monday, March 17th

Contact organizer Fuji if you would like to help
build a float, play in the band, or march in the parade!

Sammy spotted her friend Fuji putting up a notice. "Hi, Fuji!" she called happily.

"Hi, Sammy — oh no!" Fuji replied, as a sudden gust of wind blew some papers right out of her paws. "Catch those if you can!"

Sammy leaped into the air and caught one paper in her paw and another in her mouth.

"Got them!" she shouted.

First Annual
Puppyville
St. Patrick's Day
Parade

Monday, March 17th

Contact organizer Fuji if you would like to help
build a float, play in the band, or march in the parade!

"You're organizing a parade?" Sammy asked her friend. "Sounds like fun! Can I help?"

"Of course!" Fuji replied. "Do you know anyone who wants to join the band?"

"*Hmmm*, I'm not sure," Sammy replied. "But I can ask some friends. I'm on my way to dance class now. I can see if any of the puppies there are interested."

"Sounds great!" said Fuji. "Let me know!"

When Sammy got to dance class, she took her place between her friends Bridget and Gigi.

"Hi, Sammy," Bridget said. "What's new?"

"Lots!" Sammy barked excitedly. "Fuji is organizing a St. Patrick's Day parade, and she's looking for puppies to play in the band! Do you know anyone who plays an instrument?"

Bridget stretched her leg and shook her head no.

"What do you mean?" Gigi asked in surprise. "You play the bagpipes, Bridget!"

"The bagpipes?" Sammy asked. "Why, that's perfect for St. Patrick's Day. You can play in the parade!"

Bridget looked down at her paws shyly. "I just started taking lessons," she explained. "I'm really not good enough."

"You probably just need to practice more," Sammy told her friend. "Think about it."

The dance teacher, Madame Barker, clapped her paws. "Let's begin!" she said as the music started.

Bridget thought about the St. Patrick's Day parade as she danced. It would be fun to march in a parade! But she would have to practice a lot to get ready.

Sammy approached Bridget again after class.

"What do you think, Bridget?" she asked her friend. "I'm sure with some hard work, you could play in the parade. You know what they say — practice makes perfect!"

The puppies headed outside.

"I would love to be in the parade," Bridget told Sammy with a sigh. "But I don't know if I can do it. Practicing isn't much fun. I get lonely playing all by myself."

"Why don't you come to Puppyville Manor later?"
Sammy asked. "You can practice, and Gigi and I will be
your audience. Then you won't be lonely!"

"Okay," Bridget agreed. "It's worth a try!"

"*Magnifique!*" Gigi barked encouragingly. "That's the
spirit!"

Later that afternoon, Bridget practiced and Gigi and Sammy listened.

"I don't know much about bagpipes, but that sounds good to me," Sammy barked over the loud music.

"*Mmm-hmm,*" Gigi agreed, stifling a yawn. It wasn't as much fun watching someone else practice as she had thought it would be.

The door to Puppyville Manor flew open, and Fuji came in. Bridget stopped playing.

"Oh, don't stop!" Fuji exclaimed. "I hope you're getting ready for the big St. Patrick's Day parade!"

"I guess so," Bridget said halfheartedly. "But I'll have to practice a lot more to be good enough for the parade. And practicing can be boring, even if your friends are watching."

"That's it!" Sammy cried. "I've got it! Instead of sitting here watching you practice, Gigi and I should be practicing *with* you!"

"Who, *moi*?" Gigi asked in surprise. "But I don't know how to play the bagpipes!"

"I know," Sammy replied. "But you and I *do* know how to dance. We can ask Madame Barker to teach us a few Irish step dancing moves, like this."

Sammy did a little jig.

"Oh, I see!" Gigi said. "Then you and I can practice dancing while Bridget practices the bagpipes, and we can all march in the parade together!"

"That sounds like a perfect plan," Fuji agreed with a happy bark.

"*What's* a perfect plan?" Montana asked as she carried some tea into the living room to share.

"Fuji's organizing a St. Patrick's Day parade," Sammy explained. "Bridget is going to play her bagpipes, and Gigi and I are going to learn some Irish dance steps."

20

"What a great idea!" Montana said. "Sounds like you and Gigi will need some costumes. I can make them for you."

"Ooh, la la!" Gigi exclaimed. "That would be wonderful! *Merci beaucoup.* Thank you!"

That afternoon, Montana headed to the fabric store.
She picked out a pretty green fabric and got right to
work sewing dresses for Gigi and Sammy.

Meanwhile, Gigi and Sammy headed back to the
dance studio to see Madame Barker. She gave them a
quick lesson in Irish step dancing so they could head
back to Puppyville Manor to practice with Bridget.

After their lesson with Madame Barker, Sammy and Gigi practiced the dance steps over and over again while Bridget practiced the bagpipes. But she was having trouble keeping the beat.

"I'm sorry," Bridget told her friends in frustration. "Counting and playing at the same time is so hard!"

"Looks like you need a drummer," Spike replied. "I know the perfect puppy for the job. Be right back!"

A moment later, Spike returned with an empty trash can and two thick sticks.

"*Ta-da!*" he barked. "I'll be the drummer!"

"That would be great!" Bridget replied happily.

Sammy and Gigi agreed.

It was bright and sunny on St. Patrick's Day, and perfect weather for a parade. Fuji gathered her friends together and went over the route.

"Thank you all for practicing so hard to make the parade great," she told her friends. "Don't forget to have fun!"

The parade kicked off with Fuji in the lead.
Spike kept the beat while Bridget played her bagpipes.
She played better than she ever had before!

28

Gigi and Sammy wore the costumes Montana had made for them and danced the steps Madame Barker had taught them.

"This is so much fun!" Gigi said. "I'm so glad you had the idea to dance in the parade."

"Me, too!" Sammy agreed.

"You sounded great, Bridget!" Fuji told her friend.

"Thanks," Bridget replied. "Playing in the parade was the perfect way to spend St. Patrick's Day with our friends!"